BEWARE
OF BOYS

Tony Blundell

GREENWILLOW BOOKS, New York

To the wolf, without whom . . .

Text and illustrations copyright © 1991 by Tony Blundell

The moral right of the author/illustrator has been asserted.

First published in 1991 in the United Kingdom by Viking Children's Books.
First published in the United States in 1992 by Greenwillow Books.
All rights reserved. No part of this book may be reproduced or utilized in any form
or by any means, electronic or mechanical, including photocopying, recording, or by
any information storage and retrieval system, without permission in writing
from the Publisher, Greenwillow Books, a division of William Morrow & Company, Inc.,
1350 Avenue of the Americas, New York, NY 10019.   Printed at Imago in Hong Kong.
First American Edition   10 9 8 7 6 5 4 3

Library of Congress Cataloging-in-Publication Data

Blundell, Tony.
    Beware of boys / Tony Blundell.
        p.   cm.
    Summary: A small boy is captured by a wolf in
the woods and suggests some recipes for the wolf
to follow in cooking him.
    ISBN 0-688-10924-1.
    ISBN 0-688-10925-X (lib. bdg.).
    [1. Wolves—Fiction.   2. Cookery—Fiction.]
    I. Title.   PZ7.B6272Be   1992
    [E]—dc20   90-24299   CIP   AC

Once upon a time, not so very long ago, nor so very
far away, a small boy took a shortcut through
the forest . . .

. . . and was captured by a hungry wolf.

"Silly boy," said the wolf, and carried him back
to his cave.

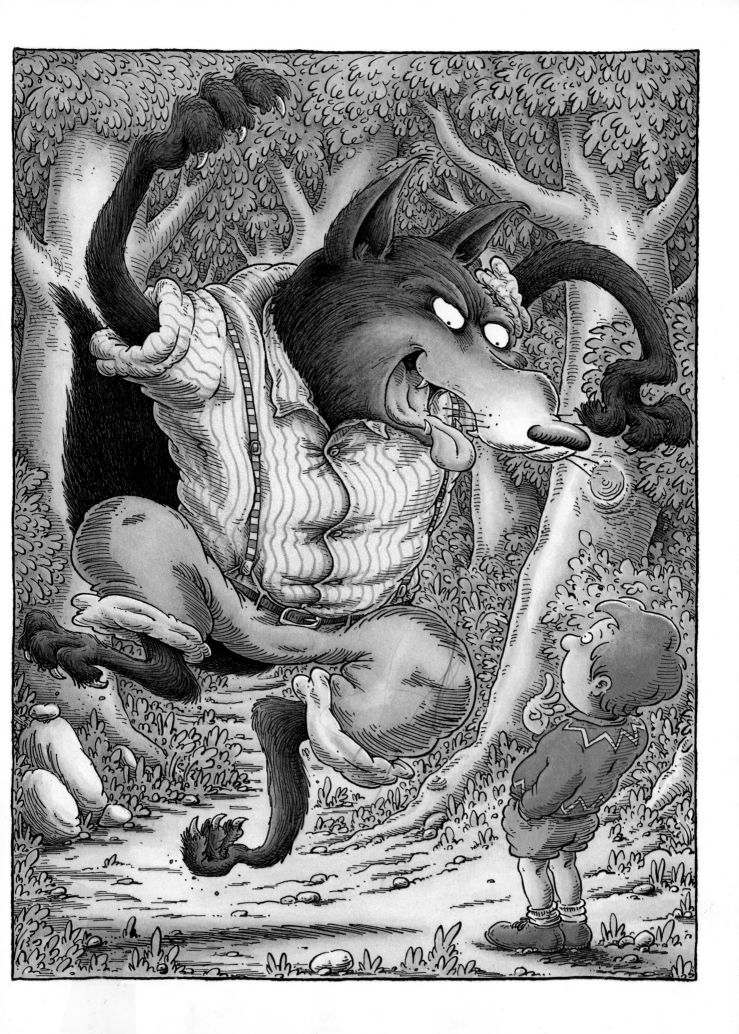

"What are you going to do with me?" asked the boy.
The wolf licked his lips. "Why, eat you, of course,"
he replied.

"Raw?" said the boy.
The wolf roared.
"No," said the boy. "I mean, aren't you even going
to cook me first?"
The wolf thought about it.

"Go on, then," he said. "What do you suggest?"

"I do just happen to know a very good recipe
for Boy Soup."
The wolf, who was both hungry and greedy, could
hardly contain himself.
"MMMMMMMMMM!" he dribbled. "Tell me what I need."
So the boy told him.

Recipe for Boy Soup

Ingredients:

(to serve one greedy wolf)

One boy (medium-sized)

One large iron pot

One ton of potatoes

One oodle of onions

One wooden tub of turnips

One cartload of carrots

One packet of fruit chews

One well-full of water

One barrel of bricks

One trowel

Method:

1. *First catch your boy.*
2. *Wash him thoroughly, especially behind the ears.*
3. *Place him firmly in the iron pot.*
4. *Add water, potatoes, onions, turnips, carrots and fruit chews to taste.*
5. *Sit on the barrel of bricks and stir with the trowel until Thursday.*

Off the wolf ran to gather the ingredients.
He raced here and there

to and fro

up and down

round and round

over and under

this way and that.

When the wolf returned, the boy checked through everything.
"Oh, silly wolf," he said. "You have forgotten the salt!"

The wolf's face fell.
"But you didn't say salt!" he spluttered.
"Well, not to worry," said the boy. "I've just remembered
an even more delicious dish which, as it happens, needs
no salt!"

The wolf's stomach started to rumble rather badly.
"Great stuff!" he said. "Tell me, tell me!"

"It's called Boy Pie," said the boy, popping a fruit chew into his mouth, "and it's three times as good as Boy Soup!"

"Yummmm!!" said the wolf.
"But you will just need a few things . . . ," said the boy.

Recipe for Boy Pie

Ingredients:
(to serve one greedy and bad-tempered wolf)

One boy (not too skinny)

One large pie dish

Three foothills of plain flour

One moo-cow of milk

One large lump of lard

Six sacks of cement

One load of leeks

One birdbath of beans

One packing case of parsnips

One shovel

One cowboy hat

One yellow yo-yo

Method:

1. Toss the flour, milk and lard with the shovel, until done.
2. Arrange the boy comfortably in the pie dish.
3. Fill his pockets with vegetables and cover with pastry.
4. Place the yo-yo in the hat and sit on it.
5. Inspect the pie hourly, then daily, until golden brown.

Off scampered the wolf.
He scurried here and there

to and fro

up and down

round and round

over and under

this way and that.

When the wolf came struggling back, huffing and puffing,
the boy examined the goods.

"Oh, wolf," he said, "silly wolf, you have forgotten the salt!"
The wolf went weak at the knees.

"But you said this one needed no salt!" he groaned.
"Well, it does," said the boy, "but never mind. I've just
remembered the most fantastically scrumptious dish that
ever was . . . and it definitely doesn't need salt!"

The wolf had almost decided on raw boy again.

He pricked up his ears.

"Go on, then," he growled. "Tell me!"

"It's called Boy Cake," said the boy, "and it's ten times better than Boy Pie!"

"And I suppose" — the wolf sighed hopelessly — "that I will just need a few things?"

"Right!" said the boy . . .

Recipe for Boy Cake

Ingredients:

(to serve one ravenously hungry and exhausted wolf)

One boy (as fat as you like)

One bathtub

One big blob of butter

One binful of brown sugar

Five fire buckets of flour

One handbag of hens' eggs

One brick outhouse

One wheelbarrow of walnuts

One shopping bag of currants

One bunch of bananas

One red bicycle

Two barn doors

One seashore of sand

One bunch of daffodils

Method:

1. *Place the boy in a warm room and allow to watch television.*
2. *Mix the butter, flour, brown sugar and hens' eggs in the bathtub.*
3. *Blend in the barn doors, bananas, currants and walnuts.*
4. *Carefully add the bicycle, sand and daffodils.*
5. *If it rains, stand in the outhouse.*

The wolf crawled off once more.
He stumbled here and there

to and fro

up and down

round and round

over and under

this way and that.

It was some time before the wolf returned, staggering under an enormous mountain of ingredients.
The boy took a long, long look.

"Oh, silly, silly wolf !" he said, shaking his head sadly.
"You have forgotten the salt."

There was a tremendous crash as the wolf collapsed.

Down went the wolf.

Down came the barn doors.

Down came the bicycle.

Down came the outhouse.

Down came the wheelbarrow, the walnuts and the currants.

Down came the fire buckets, the butter and the bin.

Down came the bananas, the hens' eggs and the sand.

Luckily, the boy managed to catch the daffodils.

The wolf lay stunned.

"Napping in the afternoon, wolf, tut-tut," said the boy,
   as he mixed together the cement, the water and the sand.

"You really should take a little more exercise," he said,
   as he placed brick upon brick, and built a wall right across
   the mouth of the wolf's cave.

"Silly old wolf," he thought, as he rode the red bicycle
   back through the forest.

When he got home, his mother was waiting for him.

"Mother, mother," he cried, "I took a shortcut through
the forest, and was captured by a hungry wolf, and
he gave me these candies, and this hat, and a new bike
. . . and he sent you these flowers!"

"He sounds nice," said his mother. "Now sit down
and eat up your supper while it's hot."

Which is more than the wolf did that night!